Copyright © 2025 by K.M. Rogness

All rights reserved.

No part of this publication may be reproduced, distributed, or transmitted in any for or by any means, including photocopying, recording or other electronic or mechanical methods, without the prior written permission of the publisher, except as permitted by U.S. Copyright law. For permission requests, contact the author by email at : darksmutauthor.km.rogness@gmail.com

The story, all names, characters, and incidents portrayed in this production are fictitious. No identification with actual persons (living or deceased), places, buildings, and products is intended or should be inferred

Cover Art: S.E. Naumann

Interior Art: Z.J. Ashton

Formatting: S.E. Naumann

Cupid's Curse

K.M. Rogness

To those who dislike Valentine's Day as much as I do, enjoy this short, smutty, *kind of funny* story. Throw your middle fingers in the air to the fat, naked baby and tell him to shove his arrow up his fucking ass.
This book is also dedicated to @blonde.and.booked for winning the title contest and for naming the two MMCS.
Stay dark, stay twisted, stay smutty! –Kasey

Blurb

Skylar, a twenty-one-year-old nonbeliever of love who swears she's been cursed by Cupid, is having a tough time this Valentine's Day. After discovering her boyfriend in bed with some chick, she vows to steer clear of all men for the foreseeable future.

With her mother embarking on a new relationship and a dinner planned to meet her boyfriend and his sons the day after Cupid vomits pink roses and candy hearts all over the world, Skylar just wants the meaningless, overplayed holiday to end.

However, a chance encounter one evening with a group of newcomers in town—some intriguing bikers—leads Skylar to accept an invitation to a Valentine's Day party, secretly hoping this might break Cupid's stupid curse once and for all.

And for one wild, euphoric night, it seems to work, and the curse placed upon her by the chubby, naked baby armed with an arrow seems to finally lift.

But when she arrives the next day to the dreadful dinner her mother planned, Skylar is confronted with a shocking twist that she never saw coming, and it makes Cupid's ridiculous curse the least of her concerns.

Content

Why choose, Darkish themes, Dark Rom-Com, Darkish Meet Cute, Cheating (not between mcs), Morally gray characters, Why choose/MFM, Independent FMC, Bikers, "One Night", Age Gap, Mistaken identity, Forbidden, Step-Siblings, Taboo, Twin brothers, One night stand, Threesomes, Mf, MFM, Valentine's Day party, Cum play, Hand Necklaces, Pierced & Tattooed MMCS, Choking, Anal play, Grumpy x sunshine, Fast Burn, Obsessive mmcs, Feisty fmc, Touch her and die, Smut-driven plot, She saves him and ends in a kind of cliffhanger.

For more of my work, check out my website: https://kmrogness.com

Chapter ONE
The Cheater

Skylar

Thud... thud... thud... thud.

Not exactly the sound I want to hear when I step into my empty apartment in the dead of night. My heart races, ready to burst from my chest. I hold my breath, quietly closing the front door before reaching for the baseball bat I keep tucked behind it. My grip tightens as I tiptoe down the hall toward the source of the noise.

It sounds like a bed slamming against the wall—like someone's having rough sex—but that can't be what's happening. Kaleb is working an overnight shift at the warehouse, and he's the only other person with a key to let himself in. Well, besides my mother, who would rather die than set foot in this part of town. She thinks it's too "ghetto" for her refined tastes.

Still holding my breath, I inch toward my bedroom door after checking the bathroom and home office, where the sound is even louder now. A sliver of light shines through the crack at the bottom of the door, tightening the lump in my throat as I grip the bat tighter, fighting the urge to bolt. I suck in a deep breath and slowly turn the knob.

Thud... thud... thud... thud...

The noise intensifies, and I close my eyes before flinging the door open, silently praying I'm not walking into my own murder. When I finally open my eyes, I'm met with a sight that makes my heart drop to the blue plush carpet beneath me: my boyfriend is on my bed, thrusting into some girl from behind, her hair in his fist, as my bed slams into the wall with each movement.

A furious heat courses through me. I rush forward, unable to utter a word as I raise the bat high. All I see is his pale, exposed ass, and I swing with all my might, the bat colliding against him like a twig snapping beneath my feet. He seizes up and topples to the side, leaving the girl panting and whining about why he stopped.

"What the hell?!" Kaleb yells in agony, his wide eyes locking onto mine as he looks back at me.

The girl's jaw drops just like mine, a deep blush creeping across her sweaty cheeks as she desperately grabs my blanket, attempting to cover herself before slipping out of my bed and pressing against the brick wall.

"Shit, Skylar, I... I... what are you doing home?" Kaleb stammers, still sprawled on the bed, his hard dick shamelessly on display.

The same dick I once loved now makes my stomach churn and I hold back the intense urge to vomit. As I lower the bat, I struggle to swallow down the nausea rising quickly within me.

"What am I doing here? In my fucking apartment? You've got to be fucking kidding," I scoff, darting a glare at the girl as she frantically tries to gather her clothes strewn across the floor.

I ignore her as I fixate on Kaleb, waiting for a response I know will amount to nothing but excuses. He just stares back at me, as if searching for a believable lie that won't come.

"I'm so sorry. I didn't know he had a girlfriend," the girl says, hastily throwing on her last piece of clothing and rushing for the door as if it's a matter of life or death—for her, no, but for Kaleb, it very well might be.

I wave her off, my attention still on Kaleb. "It's fine; he's actually single if you want him." My voice trembles, barely holding back sobs as I think of the past four years wasted on him.

She shakes her head. "No, I'm no homewrecker. I have to go." With that, she disappears like a fleeting ghost, leaving me alone with Kaleb, who remains naked but his two-inch dick is now flaccid.

Kaleb has always been a grower, not a shower. I used to assure him size didn't matter, but let's be fucking honest—size does matter, unless, and that's a big unless, the guy knows how to use it. Kaleb *clearly* doesn't.

I stride out of the room, tossing a look of disgust over my shoulder, knowing he'll trail behind me in all his nakedness. Standing by the door, I position myself just right for the motion sensor to capture what's about to unfold, knowing my cameras are about to catch everything, even his little shrimp two-inch dick.

"Skylar, please let me explain!" He begs, limping down the hallway, faux tears streaming down his face as he tries to cover his shameful excuse for a dick.

"I tried to give you a chance to explain why you were fucking some girl in our bed, but you couldn't even come up with a decent lie," I retort, swinging open the front door, pushing him out of my personal space.

With the bat in hand, I raise it again, letting it swing fiercely across his knees—those same knees that were buried in my sheets just moments ago—then I shove his naked body into the hallway. The elevator dings just then, and several of my neighbors step off, pausing mid-commute to witness the chaotic scene.

"What the fuck, Skylar? Don't do this!" He shouts, shielding his bare ass with one hand and his limp dick with the other, his cheeks burning with humiliation from the laughter of bystanders.

"You did this, Kaleb. You're the one who got caught cheating in our bed. Now you can go be with her because this shit is over between us!" I raise my middle finger and toss the bat at him, watching it bounce off the floor and inadvertently hit him right in the balls.

I can't help but laugh, using humor to stave off the tears that threaten to spill. Hell, I refuse to cry over this fucking loser. I turn my back and step inside, finally releasing the breath I'd been holding since I walked in.

Happy fucking Valentine's Day to me...

Unsure of what to do next, I retrieve my motorcycle helmet from the shelf by the door and pull on my leather jacket, craving a ride to clear my head. But just before I can leave, my phone rings, my mother's name glaring at me on the screen. I roll my eyes, holding my breath again as I answer.

"Yes, Mother?" My tone drips with attitude, knowing she'll sense something's off.

"Is this a bad time?" she whispers and mumbles something else to someone beside her.

"It's always a bad time. What do you want?"

"Well, I hope you're free tomorrow because I've made reservations for dinner. It's time you meet Kent and his sons, and I'm not taking no for an answer."

I roll my eyes, well aware she can't see me, and mimic a finger gun to my head, pretending to pull the trigger—I have no interest in her latest romantic venture, especially when I just caught mine fucking some random bitch in my fucking bed.

"I don't have shit to do for Valentine's Day or the day after, so fine, I'll meet them, but I can't promise to be on my best behavior. I'm kind of dealing with some shit right now."

She sighs, probably rolling her eyes too, whispering to whom I assume is her boyfriend. "I'm sure you'll find something to do tonight. It is Valentine's Day after all. Thank you for agreeing to dinner. I'll text you the details."

As we hang up, I glance at the clock—12:03 a.m., officially Valentine's Day, the absolute worst day of the fucking year. I pocket my phone and snatch my bike keys, stepping out into the empty hallway, my hands itching to grip the handlebars.

When I emerge into the chilly night air, I draw a shaky breath and feel hot tears slip down my cheeks. I quickly don my helmet to hide them. I refuse to waste tears on a man like him. I just want to feel the wind in my hair and the familiar vibrations of my bike beneath me. If that means riding all night to feel better, then so be it.

Swinging my leg over the seat and turning the key to start the engine, I silently vow to steer clear of all men from here on out. They aren't fucking worth it. Cupid can take his curse and his fucking arrow and shove it up his naked ass, because this Valentine's Day, it's all about me, and for once, I couldn't give two fucks about anything else.

Chapter Two
The Curse

Skylar

After riding until my legs go numb from the vibrations and my hands feel like ice in the biting wind, I coast to a stop in front of a brightly lit bar, grimacing at the sight of gaudy pink and red balloons, as well as garish neon signs proclaiming love-infused platitudes for the pointless Valentine's Day. Still, I need a fucking drink, and I need to warm up before I fucking freeze to death on my bike.

 I park right in front, setting the kickstand and locking my bike with the wheel facing the curb. I leave my helmet on the seat as I pull out a cigarette and my phone, hoping my best friend is awake and can join me for a drink.

 I shoot off a quick text and draw the smoke deep into my lungs, attention suddenly caught by an inexplicable prickling sensation along the back of my neck, as though someone is watching me.

> I'm at The Pint. Come meet me for a drink.

> That's funny, because I'm already inside. You'll see me when you walk in.

Sliding my phone into the pocket of my leather jacket, I tug up my jeans by the belt loops, ensuring my thong isn't on display when I sit down. No one needs to see my whaletail...

Snuffing out my half-finished cigarette, I exhale the smoke as I grasp the door handle and pull it open. Instantly, I'm greeted by the heady aromas of sweat, liquor, and something more primal. Of course, the Cupid Shuffle blares from the speakers, and a band of drunken idiots, mistaking their intoxication for love, clumsily attempt the dance in their boozy haze.

I scan the room and spot Luna at the end of the bar, surrounded by a gaggle of guys who look ready to devour her, their desperation almost palpable. Heads turn as I stride through the crowded space in my fitted jeans, swaying my hips deliberately; I don't bother acknowledging their stares, but I smirk straight ahead, knowing they're checking out my ass—I'd be lying if I said it doesn't make me feel good about myself, especially right now, post-breakup.

As I get near her, Luna leaps up, patting the empty seat beside her, squealing with joy and arms wide open, awaiting a hug that I'm not in the mood to give... but I give her one anyway.

"It's so... strange seeing you out... *alone*," she shouts over the pulsating music as I plop down on the stool and signal the bartender for a shot.

"Yeah, well, get used to it. Kaleb's a fucking dick, and we broke up," I reply, tossing back the tequila without the customary salt or lime, gesturing for another as my gaze locks onto the handsome bartender just a few feet away.

"You... you broke up?!" Her eyes widen, mirroring my own shock when I caught Kaleb in the act with that other woman.

I nod, filling her in on the details between shots, a warm buzz enveloping me before long. By the time I've poured out my heart, she looks ready to fight, and knowing Luna, she could easily take Kaleb on with a grin and wet painted nails and still win.

"I can't fucking believe he cheated on you," she sighs, shaking her head as she pushes away the cluster of guys circling her like she's their prey.

"It is what it is. I don't want to dwell on it. I just want to get fucking drunk and just... be me, I guess." I down shot number five, blissfully numb to the burn it leaves behind, thinking back on the last four years and how much of them were a fucking waste of time.

A mischievous sparkle ignites in Luna's brown eyes, and I brace myself for the trouble she's likely plotting for me tonight.

"What's that look for?" I ask warily, preparing for the inevitable nonsense about to unfold.

"You need to get laid. Like a no-strings-attached one-night stand," she smirks, set on breaking whatever Cupid's curse has me ensnared in.

I shake my head, unwilling; but deep down, I know I could use the distraction—it's been too long since I felt any form of release, because, let's face it, Kaleb sucked at making me come, and most of the time I'd have to finish myself off because his ass was a two-pump chump. Why I was with him for so long is beyond me. But the sad thing is I don't know who I am without him. We became one in the years we were together, losing our identities, which is the reason I have no idea who I am now.

"It's Valentine's Day, girl. You absolutely have to get laid," she laughs, gesturing dramatically around the bar at the assortment of possibilities, her tight blonde curls bouncing against her shoulders as she laughs.

"It's the early morning of Valentine's Day; that doesn't count. If I'm going to hook up, it'll be when everyone else is doing lovey-dovey shit and being all sappy tonight."

"There's a party down by the train tracks in that old warehouse; I hear it's supposed to be ahh-mazing," she says while sipping her martini, her demeanor more posh than either of us truly are.

"I might check it out. It's not like I have any plans," I chuckle at my own plight, masking my melancholy with laughter to stave off the tears that threaten to surface.

Glancing up, I catch the bartender staring at me; an unreadable twinkle in his eye that lets face it makes me hot between my thighs. I nod, giving off a flirtatious yet subtle grin as I twirl a strand of hair around my finger. He smiles wider, focusing on me while drying a beer mug, oblivious to the world around us. I don't know who he is, but I'm sure I'll find out sooner than later. His eyes alone are enough to get me fucking pregnant, so I already know I need to stay away from him.

One of the guys Luna was with when I arrived sidles back, asking her to dance. She gives me a worried look, hesitant to leave me alone, but I nod encouragingly for her to go have fun. I'll be just fine here at the bar, surrounded by drinks and hot men all around me.

After far too many shots to keep track, the pressing urge to pee ambushes me. With Luna lost in a dance with another guy, I hop off the stool and weave through the crowd to the back of the bar, squinting against the relentless flashing lights.

Just as I'm about to push open the bathroom door, I collide with a tall stranger I've never encountered before. His striking green eyes pierce into mine, stealing my breath away. He towers over me, easily six feet tall, looking down into my bloodshot, drunken gaze, a dazzling grin lighting up his face as dimples deepen in his cheeks.

His dark curls flop into his eyes, and with a quick, smooth Bieber motion—like a puppy shaking off water—he sweeps them aside, his stare intensifying as he steps closer, igniting a thrill in my chest.

"Wow, you're stunning," he blurts out, unabashed in his flattery.

"Uh, thanks," I stammer, hiccuping mid-sentence.

My eyes wander over him—his black shirt clings to his torso, revealing powerful biceps adorned with ink that wraps around his arms and neck in intricate designs. I find myself tracing the curves and lines, imagining the treasures hiding beneath his clothing.

His gaze flicks down my body, lingering for a moment before he meets my eyes again with a knowing grin, a brow arched, and that irresistibly sexy set of dimples on display. I clear my throat, trying to recover, as if I weren't just undressing him with my gaze.

"Nice ink," he says, gesturing to the tattoos peeking out from my top, covering the area just above my tits, the only skin I have exposed.

"Thanks, yours are great too," I reply, tucking a stray strand of hair behind my ear as heat floods my cheeks from his relentless gaze tracking from my feet to my eyes.

"What's your name, pretty girl?" He asks, his tone playful, stirring something deep within me.

"Sky… Skylar," I stutter, momentarily forgetting my own name under the spell of his allure.

He nods and sensuously licks his lips, revealing a barbell piercing, which sends a rush of warmth pooling low.

"Beautiful name for a beautiful girl," he says smoothly, coaxing an involuntary smile from my lips.

"Thank you…?" I trail off, eagerly awaiting the revelation of his name.

"My bad, I'm—" he starts, but the escalating music drowns out the rest.

I don't dare request a repeat. I simply nod and smile, moving closer to the bathroom door, caught in a daze until I find myself unexpectedly rising on my tiptoes and pressing my glossy lips to his. He kisses me back, momentarily stunned, before pulling away, shock etched across his striking features. A wave of embarrassment washes over me instantly.

"I'm sorry, I didn't mean to—" Before he can finish the denial, I cut him off, shaking my head dismissively.

"Shit, my bad. I don't know what I was thinking," I blurt, mortification flooding through me like a tidal wave.

Without waiting for his response, I rush past him and dive into the bathroom, locking myself in a stall, the heat of embarrassment coursing through me.

Fuck. This curse is no joke, and it's fucking everything up. Besides, I'm not nearly drunk enough for this shit.

I'm not sure how long I end up hiding out in the bathroom stall, but by the time I dare show my face in the bar, the tall, handsome stranger is gone, and I'm able to breathe a sigh of relief as I make my way back to Luna and the gorgeous bartender with the same green eyes as the hottie I just fucking kissed.

"Where did you disappear to?" she asks, wiggling her perfect brows as if hinting at a hookup, to which I frantically shake my head no.

"Uh, the bathroom, yeah. I think I'm going to head out," I tell her, tossing a few crisp bills on the bar for my drinks, slipping my arms back into my jacket.

I'm not quite ready to brave the cold again, but I know I need to get out of here before I make another fool out of myself. I hug Luna and say my goodbyes, my eyes darting nervously around the sea of dancing people.

As I turn to walk away, I collide with a firm chest, feeling cold liquid soak through my white top as the sound of glass shatters as it hits the ground. Looking through fluttering lashes, I see the same guy I kissed standing in front of me, wearing the same drink that I am but with a smirk on his face while a look of horror washes over mine.

"So we meet again... I wouldn't peg you for such a clumsy person, Skylar," he teases, turning my cheeks bright red.

"My bad. I'm so sorry," I stammer, gripping my bike key extra tightly as if it's a magical trinket that'll take me to a faraway place—anywhere away from here.

Without waiting for another word to be spoken between us, I run out of the bar, saying fuck the cold because I just embarrassed myself for the second time tonight in front of the same man.

Cupid's Curse is no fucking joke. That naked baby must really have it out for me.

The chill of the night air hits me like a slap in the face and puts my hard, pointy nipples on display through my wet shirt as I step further outside, but I hardly care; I just need to get away. My breath comes out in frosty clouds, mingling with the remnants of tequila still swirling in my belly.

I start trudging toward my bike, my mind a tangled mess of adrenaline and embarrassment, desperately attempting to suppress the memories of tonight's cringe-worthy moments.

Then I hear a voice calling my name. "Skylar!"

I look back, and there he is—Green Eyes, the same handsome stranger, now hastily pushing through the bar's door, his tousled curls dancing in the night breeze. His eyes lock onto mine, that cocky smirk still very much in place, and I both want to crawl into a hole and simultaneously throw myself at him. But as those thoughts swirl, I know one thing is certain: I can't deal with this right now, not after what just fucking happened.

"I wasn't finished talking to you!" he exclaims, closing the distance between us.

With each step closer, I feel my pulse quicken. The warmth from the bar, the noise, the laughter—all of it seems to dissolve into the background, leaving only me and him standing tense in the cold.

"Look, um, I'm really not in the mood to—"

He interrupts me, his green eyes softening. "I know I wasn't exactly what you wanted to be dealing with after a rough night, but I still owe you an introduction."

"Well, technically, you didn't get to finish your last one since I, uh, well, you know," I mutter, waving a hand dismissively, feeling heat rise to my cheeks yet again.

"Yeah, about that." He pauses, running a hand through his hair. "I didn't exactly see that coming. Didn't know I had such an effect on you." There's that smirk again, and I want to roll my eyes, but instead I just want to melt into the fucking pavement.

"I'm really sorry," I murmur, wishing that I could disappear. "Honestly, I'm not like that. It was just a weird moment due to a really bad fucking day."

"Who says weird moments can't lead to something good, especially after a bad fucking day?" He raises an eyebrow, his expression turning thoughtful. "I'm Kallen, by the way."

"Kallen," I repeat. It sounds good, rolling off my tongue, but I'm not sure I can handle the charms of a man like him right now. "So, um... what are you doing out here in the freezing cold?"

"I was gonna ask you the same. But I can definitely think of a warmer place where we could talk more," he suggests, glancing back toward the bar as if he might turn me around and lead me into the chaos.

"Look, Kallen, I really need to leave," I insist, feeling my heart race at the thought of prolonging this awkward exchange. Still, deep down, something is stirring—a small glimmer of curiosity, of possibility.

"Or," he lowers his voice, leaning closer so I can catch the scent of his cologne, "you could let loose and have some fun for a change. It's Valentine's Day, after all."

He shoves his hands into the pockets of his jeans as a delightful grin creeps back on his face. For a moment, I imagine what it would be like to have someone like him holding me close, and the warmth that blooms in my chest tells me just how much I crave human connection that doesn't involve heartache.

"I don't know." I hedge, glancing back at my bike, the thought of that cold seat making dread pool in my gut.

"Just one drink. No strings attached." His voice is smooth and persuasive, enough to make it hard to refuse when I've been so lonely tonight.

I take a deep breath and weigh my options. I could ride home, wallow in my thoughts, and reinforce the idea that I'm not worth risking further embarrassment. Or I could take a leap, and if it goes sideways, I can always tell myself it'll just add to the night's collection of awkward memories.

"Okay," I say, my voice barely above a whisper as the word forms from my lips like a commitment I didn't know I was making. "One drink."

"Perfect," Kallen replies, his smile lighting up the night as he gestures toward the bar.

I pull my jacket tighter around me, caught in the uncertainty of what the night could hold, and for the first time in too long, I feel the shadows of my heart grow lighter. I might have kissed him too soon; I might have embarrassed myself; hell, I might be risking another stumble tonight, but something whispers that breaking free from Cupid's Curse may start with one wild decision to try again.

Chapter THREE
The Fling

Skylar

One fucking drink... yeah, right.

One drink flows effortlessly into another, and as the evening unfolds, all our cares and inhibitions are cast aside. Kallen pushes me against my front door as we stumble into my apartment, our lips locked in a fervent embrace. Our tongues dance in a passionate duel, each of us determined to claim dominance in a battle neither of us is willing to concede.

His strong hands glide down my sides, landing on my ass, where he cups it firmly and lifts me, using the door as support. My back presses into the wood, the doorknob digging uncomfortably into my tailbone, yet the intoxication of his kiss makes the pain fade into the background. I know it will linger tomorrow, but for tonight, all I want is to feel every inch of him against me.

"Let me in," he murmurs seductively against my lips, urging me to surrender control of the kiss.

And oh, how I'm glad I did.

He teases me, swirling his tongue around mine, his fingers sinking into the soft curves of my body as I pull him closer, pressing our bodies flush against one another as we break free from the door's confines.

In the dim light, we navigate the hallway to my room, our mouths never parting. He gently lays me on my bed, his body following suit, cascading down to rest atop mine. His hands explore my body like a blind man reading an intricate map, sending delicious shivers coursing through me, igniting a heat I've never experienced before—not even with shrimp-dick Kaleb.

As we roll together on the bed, our clothes begin to vanish, our lips parting only long enough to shed each layer before reconnecting with fervor. We delve into each other's mouths as if they hold the secrets to hidden treasures that we're both so desperate to find.

Somehow, I find myself naked on top of Kallen, leaning down to press a kiss to the side of his neck. His hand shoots up to playfully grasp mine, teasingly squeezing as I grind against him, feeling him grow harder and rise, pressing against the slick warmth between my trembling thighs.

"Fuck, you're soaked," he whispers as he nips at my earlobe, making my body tremble even more than my thighs as his cock continues to prod at my entrance.

"What can I say?" I flirt back, raking my black acrylic nails down his beautifully tattooed chest, making him let out a grunt of approval as he reaches his free hand behind me and begins to knead my ass like dough.

"Guess you just know how to get me going." I breathe against his ear, savoring the way his breath hitches just a little.

He suddenly flips me onto my back, hovering over me while staring into my eyes, my hands gliding up and down his muscular back. There's something intoxicating about this moment—the thrill of our bodies colliding, the sweet desperation simmering between us. I feel powerful, and I want him to know that, more than I ever wanted anyone—especially Kaleb—to know.

With a sudden burst of confidence, I shift my weight and flip us over, again straddling him with my knees planted firmly on either side of his hips. The surprise in his eyes morphs into admiration, as if he's just realized how fiercely I could take control. I lean down, capturing his lips in a heated kiss once more, my body grinding against his. I can feel the heat radiating between us, charging the air with electricity.

"Looks like somebody's finally feeling bold," he chuckles, the warmth of his voice sending shivers down my spine.

"Just keeping up with you," I tease, focusing on the way his chest rises and falls beneath me.

I sit up slightly, relishing the view. His dark hair tousled and damp, his body glistening in the low light—Kallen looks every bit the dangerous man I've always found so irresistible.

I lean back a little, teasingly dragging my nails along the sensitive skin of his thighs, savoring each gasp and groan he releases. His eyes darken with desire, and I can't help but bite my lip in anticipation. I want him to lose himself in this moment, to succumb entirely to the madness we're creating together.

"Tell me what you want," he urges, voice low and rough. There's a challenge in his gaze, one that compels me to push further.

I smirk, glancing down at him with playful defiance. "I want you to make me feel good. Really fucking good."

The moment I say those words, Kallen's hands find my waist, and he flips us again, bringing me back beneath him. He hovers above me, dominating the space, his breath warm against my collarbone. "Is that an order?"

"Maybe," I whisper, encouraging him with a tilt of my hips, longing for the friction that my body craves.

"Good, because I aim to please," he replies, his lips wrapping around my nipple, sending shockwaves of pleasure through me.

I arch my back, urging him to continue, to explore, to unleash the primal need that's been boiling inside me ever since we bumped into each other the first time.

His mouth moves lower, trailing down my stomach as he drinks me in, each kiss igniting my skin with fire. He stops just above my throbbing core, looking up at me with those intoxicating eyes—challenging, hungry, and filled with a promise.

"Are you ready? Cus I'm fucking starving," he asks, and I nod frantically, every part of me screaming for what's to come.

With a knowing smile, he delivers, and I'm plunged into a world of ecstasy as he takes his time, teasing and teasing, until I feel like I might explode. The room becomes a blur of moans, gasps, and heated whispers, the night stretching long before us—a tapestry painted with raw passion and the urgency of youth.

His pierced tongue laps up the wetness he has coaxed from me, making his lips and chin glisten as he comes up just to make a show of licking my arousal off them. And then he dives back down, plunging his tongue inside of me while his fingers dig into my thighs as he pushes them open wider.

I reach down and tug on his curls, pressing his mouth firmly against my pussy as he continues to eat me like a five-course meal, my legs quivering as the muscles in my lower belly tighten from the pleasure.

Every flick of his tongue sends shockwaves through me, our bodies performing an intoxicating dance fueled by the heat of desire and the sweet nectar of my need. I arch my back, losing myself in the moment, completely at the mercy of Kallen's hungry mouth. My moans fill the room, a symphony of pleasure that echoes off the walls, urging him on as he effortlessly brings me closer to the edge.

"God, Kallen... yes," I moan breathlessly, my fingers tightening in his hair, and he responds with a growl that sends a fresh wave of pleasure coursing through me.

He relishes the taste of my desire, his determination unwavering as he buries his face deeper, setting a rhythm that makes me pant and writhe beneath him.

"Can't get enough of you," he murmurs against my sensitive skin before tugging on my clit, the vibrations sending violent jolts of ecstasy throughout my body.

He looks up at me, those dark eyes filled with an insatiable hunger, as he resumes his ministrations. Each push and swirl of his tongue is deliberate and calculated, driving me wild with an intensity I've never known.

"Don't stop," I plead, breathless and frantic. "I'm so close..."

He responds by picking up the pace, giving me everything I need, and then some, his fingers now circling my clit with a deftness that makes my hips buck uncontrollably. I can feel that familiar tightening in my core, the sweet anticipation of release building to an unbearable crescendo. I gasp, my body quivering as he expertly pulls me closer, teetering on the precipice of pure bliss.

The world begins to fade beyond the sensation of him—my breathing, his touch, the burning need that consumes me—until it all explodes into a galaxy of light and sound. My back arches off the bed as pleasure washes over me, crashing like waves against the shore. I cry out Kallen's name, shattering my own sense of control as the waves of ecstasy carry me away.

As I tumble back into reality, he shifts back up my body, his lips curling into a satisfied smile. "Told you I aim to please." There's a glint of mischief in his eyes, and I can't help but return his grin despite the delicious haze clouding my senses.

"Fucking hell," I manage to muster, still catching my breath. "That was incredible."

"Just wait till you see what else I can do," he murmurs, his voice low and sultry as he moves, prompting me to inhale sharply in anticipation. "I've only just begun."

Before I can respond, he claims my lips once more, his kiss heating back up as our bodies instinctively reconnect. I can taste myself on him—a raw reminder of how he brings out this wild side of me. But Kallen's not done yet; his hands rove my body with a fierce urgency, reigniting the fire that hadn't even had a chance to dim.

As our kisses deepen, I become hyper-aware of him—his warmth spreading through me, his heartbeat drumming a steady rhythm against my skin, the way his fingers lace through my hair as if holding onto this moment for dear life. It's intoxicating, and I crave more.

"Let's go again," I whisper, grinning challengingly as I pull him closer, feeling every hard inch of him against me. The hunger in his eyes mirrored my own, a promise of even more to come.

With that, Kallen knows exactly what I mean. The air is electric as he nods, hands firmly gripping my waist once more. In one swift motion, he flips us again—this time, I'm pinned beneath him but on my knees with my ass in the air, his massive cock poking into it, yet excitedly liberated by the change. The thrill of him being in control electrifies the atmosphere, dissolving the world around us until there's only us—our bodies, our desires, the insatiable dance of intimacy burning brightly like fire.

Kallen's expressions deepen, and with every second, the connection between us strengthens, transcending the boundaries within the chaotic whirlwind we've crafted. The night stretches endlessly ahead as he slides into me with desperation, my pussy molding around his cock, and with every thrust, every kiss, I know we're spiraling deeper into this wild oblivion where nothing else matters—just the two of us in this intimate chaos.

He pushes on my lower back, putting me at the perfect angle for him to thrust in and out as deep as he can go. His hand grabs a fistful of my hair, and he tugs roughly, jerking my head up and back while firmly gripping my throat, giving me the best hand necklace I've ever gotten.

His thrusts are wild and demanding, my bed thumping into the wall as he fucks me harder, my tits bouncing beneath me and my nipples grazing the sheet, giving me another chill. But he doesn't let up. He goes harder and deeper, ripping moans and sounds I've never heard coming from my throat, and all I want is more.

I feel like I'm unraveling in his grip, lost in the rhythm of our bodies meeting over and over again. His deep growls of pleasure resonate against my back, sending jolts of excitement through me with each thrust. I can tell he's losing himself, too—his movements become erratic, driven by a primal need that echoes my own. It's intoxicating, and it drives me fucking wild.

"God, yes," I gasp, my voice raw with desire. "Just like... fuck, just like that."

Kallen responds by tightening his hold on my hair and throat, exerting a delicious control that makes my heart race. Every time he fills me completely, the world outside disappears, and all that exists is the heady connection between us. I rock my hips back against him, reveling in the feeling of him stretching me and claiming me.

"Your body is fucking perfect," he growls lowly, punctuating his words with another deep thrust that makes me moan louder.

The sensation leaves me breathless, and I can feel the tension building deeper within my core, an insatiable longing that begs for release.

"Please—don't stop," I whimper, daring to glance back over my shoulder, meeting his smoldering gaze.

There's a fierce intensity in his eyes, the kind that ignites my body and convinces me he wants this just as much as I do.

His grip on my throat loosens slightly, and I can breathe again, though the heat of his body pressing against mine is almost suffocating in the best way. Kallen lets go of my hair, sliding his hand down my back and wrapping it around my waist, driving me closer with every powerful thrust.

"You want it harder, pretty girl?" he asks, his voice dripping with challenge. The fire in his gaze promises that he can give me everything I crave, and my heart hammers in response.

"Yes!" I cry, pushing my hips back against his, eager for more. "I want it so bad."

With a low growl, he obliges, increasing the tempo and the intensity. The sound of skin slapping against skin and our ragged breaths fill the room, mingling together in a primal symphony. Each thrust reverberates through me, stirring sensations I never knew existed, pulling me closer to the precipice I'm dying to leap from.

"Fuck—you feel so good," he pants, his fingers digging into my hips as he drives deeper. "You're mine, you know that?"

The possessive statement sends thrills coursing through me, heightening the pleasure and giving me a sense of belonging I didn't know I was missing.

"I'm yours, Kallen. All yours," I breathe a lie, lost in the madness that has enveloped us.

"Good," he replies with a fierce smile, and then he angles his thrusts to hit the sweet spot deep inside me, forcing me to cry out again as stars dance behind my eyelids. I feel the tension peak, bubbling just beneath the surface and ready to overflow.

"Almost there," I manage to whisper, desperation lacing my words. "Just a little more!"

He responds by slamming into me harder than before, the sound of our bodies colliding echoing around the room. I feel every inch of his cock—a rush of heat, pressure, and pleasure that builds until I'm consumed by it. I cling to the sheets, my body arching helplessly as I spin closer to the edge.

"Let go, pretty girl," he urges, his voice low and filled with urgency. "I want to feel you come all over my cock."

With those words, I tumble over the brink, spiraling into nothingness as my body explodes with pleasure. I scream his name, my muscles tightening around him as the waves of ecstasy roll through me, taking every ounce of breath with them. I feel him plunge deeply, riding the waves of my release as he finds his own, filling me with a warmth that sends shivers through my entire being.

We're both breathless, collapsing onto the bed together, our bodies tangled and slick with sweat as we try to regain our sense of reality. Kallen smiles down at me, his gaze filled with satisfied hunger, his chest rising and falling against mine.

"I knew you were fucking trouble the moment we met," he whispers, brushing a thumb over my cheek.

And for the first time in a long time, I don't mind being in trouble. In fact, I revel in it, and as I pull him down for another kiss, the night stretches before us—full of endless possibilities and untouched desires waiting to ignite once more.

I think Cupid's curse has lifted, and I can feel my lips break into a smile as Kallen wraps me into his body, my ass firmly pressed against his cock as we lie on my bed trying to catch our breath.

Chapter Four

The Hitchiker

Skylar

Valentine's Day evening

Awakening to the fading light of a Valentine's Day almost entirely spent asleep, I groan, my body protesting the intense workout from the previous night, every muscle throbbing and on fire from being used in ways they haven't in a long fucking time. Immediately my thoughts drift back to last night with Kallen, and a smile forces its way across my lips, making my cheeks hurt.

I look down, noticing only a thin t-shirt clinging to my chest, not even long enough to cover my naked ass or the bite marks and bruises left behind by Kallen. When I stretch, I instantly regret it; the pain from moving my body is much worse.

"Oww," I whine, swinging my legs over the edge of my bed, the blinking notification light on my phone catching my eye.

"What the fuck now?" I mumble, yanking it off the charger, which backfires when the long braided cable retaliates and smacks me right in the mouth.

I already want to go back to sleep until this day is over. Nothing good ever comes from Valentine's Day, and it's already proving to be true when I open my phone and see many missed calls and text messages from Kaleb, whose name in my phone is now shrimp dick. Not wanting to deal with his bullshit, I delete all twelve messages without even reading them. But just as they finish moving to the trash, another one pops across my screen, and the preview of the message informs me that he's on his way over so we can talk.

No, the fuck we're not.

I bolt out of bed, accepting the aching all throughout my body, and dash to my closet to quickly get dressed. Staying away from red and pink, I grab a blue lacy crop top and a pair of black jeans with rips in the knees. I don't think I've ever gotten dressed so fast. But I'll be fucking damned if I'm still here when that asshole shows up.

I apply a quick layer of mascara and eyeliner, run a brush through my hair, and brush my teeth, trying not to drip toothpaste onto my shirt. When I'm done and satisfied with my appearance, I run down the hallway, sliding in my socks across the shiny hardwood floor, almost colliding with the end table near the front door.

Lucky no one is here to see me almost bust my ass.

I grab my leather jacket and step into my riding boots, just wanting to take a ride to clear my head.

Once I put my helmet on, my anxiety fades, and the nerves in my belly dissipate. I rush out of my apartment, feeling hidden from the world, but mainly knowing that even if I were to bump into Kaleb, his ass wouldn't recognize me since he never paid attention to the color of my helmet or anything for that matter.

I step into the elevator, sliding my phone in the zipper pocket in my jacket, feeling it vibrate almost instantly. But I ignore it, just wanting out of this building as fast as I can. The second the elevator doors slide open and I step off, I see Kaleb walking toward me, a bouquet of pink and red roses in his hand. I cringe, walking casually as if I'm no one to him, which, let's face it, I'm not anymore.

I walk past him and subtly turn to look over my shoulder, watching him step into the elevator with no fucking clue that it was me who just walked by him. It just goes to show how much he paid attention for the years we were together. Another reason I'm glad I walked away from his sorry ass.

The sun has fully set by the time I get to my bike, mounting it slowly because of the pain in my legs from Kallen spreading them as if I were a fucking gymnast. The growl from the engine and the vibrations against my inner thighs awaken me, putting me completely at ease as I take off in the night, the crisp wind in my hair, and the bright full moon following me as I ride.

The city lights blur into streaks of color as I accelerate, the rhythmic thump of the engine a soothing counterpoint to the throbbing ache in my muscles. The wind whips through my hair, a welcome distraction from the lingering tension of the encounter—or rather, the non-encounter—with Kaleb. He'd probably be fucking fuming, oblivious to the fact that he just missed me. A small, wicked smile plays on my lips. Serves him fucking right.

My phone vibrates again, insistent in its silence within my jacket pocket. I ignore it, letting the speed and the freedom of the ride wash over me. The pain in my legs is a dull throb now, overshadowed by the exhilaration of the open road. The moon, a brilliant silver disc in the inky sky, seems to guide me, its light reflecting off the wet asphalt.

I ride for hours, the miles melting away beneath my wheels. The city gives way to winding country roads, the air cleaner, the silence punctuated only by the purr of my engine, and the occasional chirp of a cricket. I find a secluded spot overlooking a valley, the lights of distant houses twinkling like fallen stars. I switch off the engine, the sudden quiet almost deafening after the constant hum.

Leaning against my bike, I pull out my phone, finally checking the barrage of messages. Most are from Kaleb, increasingly frantic and desperate. One is a picture of the roses, wilting already. I delete them all without a second thought.

There's also a text from Kallen, a simple

> "Evening, sleepyhead. Hope you're not too sore."

A warm feeling spreads through me, chasing away the lingering chill of the night.

I reply with a quick

> Evening, fucker. Sore but happy.

Then, I add,

> See you tonight?

The reply is almost instantaneous

> Tonight there's a Valentine's Day party at the bar. I was sorta hoping I could take you.

> Fine, I'll go, but just so you know, I fucking hate this holiday, so don't expect me to be dressed all pretty in pink and shit.

> Just get your ass to the fucking bar.

A grin stretches across my face. Tonight is going to be a very long night. And with my utter hatred for the pointless holiday, if it means I have another opportunity to see Kallen, I guess I can deal with it for a few hours.

I start the engine, the familiar growl a promise of more adventures to come, and head back towards the city, the moon still my silent companion, the night still young, and my heart full of a different kind of ache—the good kind.

Not even a mile away from the bar, I spot a fellow biker stranded on the side of the road, his arm stretched out with his thumb up, signaling he's looking for a ride. Being the nice bitch that I am, I pull over, stopping my bike in front of his and climbing off once the kickstand is down.

I keep my helmet on but flip the visor up as I approach him. He turns his head and puts his arm down, lifting his visor, a familiar yet distant twinkle in his eyes making my breath hitch.

"I hate to state the obvious, but I take it somethings fucked with your bike and you need a ride?" I ask, scanning his bright red bike, shiny enough to see my reflection.

The look he gives me is one of shock; even just by looking at his eyes, the only part of him I can see. He wasn't expecting some chick to pull over and save the day, but guess what? It looks like I am.

"Yeah, shit won't stay running. I thought it was the gas, but the tank's still about halfway full," he says, still piercing his eyes into mine. "I was heading to this party at some bar down the street. You think you can give me a lift. I'm not from around here, so I don't know where the fuck I'm going."

I laugh, a little surprised he's going to the same spot as me, but in a small town, it's usually the place where everyone goes.

"The Pint, right?" I ask, running my hand over his bike, savoring the touch of the smooth finish.

"Yeah, you know it?" He takes his key out of the ignition and pockets it, doing a quick check to make sure he has everything he needs.

"Sure do. Matter of fact, I'm heading there myself." I smile even though he can't see it, but my eyes squint, giving him the faintest hint of one that he returns, a low chuckle leaving his chest. "Come on, I don't mind giving you a ride."

I turn to walk back to my bike, feeling his eyes burning straight into my ass, even without having to turn around. I swing my leg over the seat and inch forward so there's room for him.

"I'm Roman," he announces as he climbs on behind me, his hand gripping the sides of my bike instead of wrapping his arms around me.

Which, let's face it, I'd rather anyway since I have no idea who this fucking man is. For all I know, I could end up on the side of the road, dead in a ditch, before we even get to the bar. But that wouldn't even be the worst part. The worst part would be that I was murdered on fucking Valentine's Day, the day I despise the most.

"I'm Skylar," I reply, closing my visor and then gripping the handlebars, feeling better than I have in a long fucking time all because me, some little biker chick, came to a grown ass man's rescue. Shit, it makes me feel good.

With the engine rumbling to life beneath me, I pull smoothly back onto the road, my heart racing not just from the thrill of the ride but from the intriguing presence behind me. I can feel Roman's energy—a mix of excitement and a hint of recklessness—radiating against my back. It's fucking intoxicating.

"Hold on tight!" I shout over the roar of the engine, the world around us blurring once more.

I lean into the curves, my instincts taking over as I maneuver through the occasional potholes and sudden turns, navigating toward the bar that pulses with the nightlife of the city. The night air rushes past, cool and refreshing, and despite my usual disdain for Valentine's festivities, there's a thrill simmering inside me. The sheer act of speed and freedom envelops me like a favorite song I haven't heard in ages. Roman's presence—with his newfound energy and those easy, breezy vibes—adds a new layer to my ride, making it one of the most enjoyable evenings I've had in a long time.

As we approach The Pint, I can see the neon lights glowing like a beacon, drowning out the darkness surrounding it. The thumping bass from inside spills over into the street, a reminder of what awaits. I slow down and pull to a stop, cutting the engine. The sudden silence plunges us back into reality.

Roman swings his leg over, dismounting gracefully before he steps around to where I am. I pull off my helmet, tugging at my hair to get rid of the messy nest it has become. Roman keeps his helmet on as he pulls out his phone, I assume calling someone to take care of his bike.

"Wow," he says, cracking a smirk. "You really know how to handle that bike."

I roll my eyes, unable to hide the blush creeping up my cheeks. "It's just a bike, but thanks. You're not too bad yourself for a runaway roadside hitchhiker."

"Oh, I don't know about that. I had my doubts when a badass chick like you showed up to rescue me," he responds, his eyes lighting up as his grin spreads wider. "But I'm glad I took my chances."

I chuckle and step closer to him, drawn into his magnetic presence. "Well, let's see if you're still glad after we've both had a few drinks. Might find out I'm more trouble than I look."

"Ah, trouble can be fun," Roman quips, his eyes dancing with a hint of mischief. "Care for a drink to celebrate my rescue?"

At the mention of drinks and the festive atmosphere of the bar, I remember Kallen and the invitation from earlier, still lingering in my mind. But the thought of partying with him—while still tempting—fades slightly as I look at Roman, who seems genuinely eager to have a good time. Earth's world doesn't have to revolve around just one man after all.

"Sure, why not? Just don't blame me when I show you how to really have fun on a holiday everyone hates," I challenge. I'll meet you inside, though. I have to take a piss," I admit bluntly, causing him to laugh.

"Alright, I'll be right in. I have to make a call," he says, leaning against my bike.

I salute him as I walk to the door, anxiously pulling it open, secretly wishing Kallen is already here. Inside, the ambiance is electric. Couples are dancing, laughter bounces off the walls, and the air is thick with the scent of spilled beer and overwhelming perfume. I wave at the bartender, a familiar face that I've seen before, as I make my way past the bar toward the bathroom.

I smile to myself as I think of the night I met Kallen as I push open the bathroom door, memories of our wild night together still fresh in my mind. While doing my business, I shoot Kallen a text, letting him know that I'm here and that I'll be waiting at the bar. Of course, he replies instantly with an "Okay, see you soon."

I wash my hands when I'm done, touching up my hair and appearance as I glance in the mirror at my hot mess self. Gliding my chapstick on my lips, my phone startles me, vibrating in my pocket and making me jump. Also making my hand slip and my chapstick coat a layer up my cheek. Thank fuck it's clear and not lipstick or something. I wipe it off and pull out my phone, dreadfully answering a call from my lovely mother.

"Yeah?"

"Jesus, Skylar, could you sound anymore annoyed? And how rude to answer the phone that way," she gasps, and I roll my eyes at her, wishing she could see through the fucking phone.

"Sorry, mother. What can I assist you with this blissful evening?"

"Smartass," she snaps, again whispering to someone who's with her. "I'm just calling to remind you about dinner tomorrow night. I made reservations at the place you like on the water."

"Ma, it's fucking dead ass winter. Why the fuck would I want to eat on a fucking deck in the damn cold?" This time I snap, regretting agreeing to join her.

"We have a table indoors; relax. Are you still coming?"

"Yeah, I'll be there."

"Good, Kent is really excited to meet you," she says, her tone switching to cheerful in the blink of an eye.

"Yeah, okay, great. I'll see you guys tomorrow," I mutter, ending the call before she can blab about anything else.

I need a fucking drink.

Stepping out of the bathroom, I anxiously make my way through the crowd, just wanting to get to the bar. I don't see Roman, but I see Kallen, his back to me as his head turns to look at the crowd. I sneak up behind him and pinch his ass, making him jump. And then my arms wrap around his waist, and I rise on my toes to whisper in his ear.

"Nice ass, you wanna have a quickie out back?" I joke, laughing as he slowly turns around.

And then my jaw drops. Something isn't right.

Roman looks at me, his eyes wide in shock, but a mischievous grin plays along his lips. The shock of his dark hair against his tanned skin makes me hesitate. His eyes—the same intriguing twinkle that caught my attention earlier—now flash with appreciation and curiosity. But that isn't what's wrong. It's the fact that he looks exactly like—

"There you are," Kallen comes up from behind me, grabbing my hip and tugging me backwards so my ass fits against his groin like a puzzle piece.

I do a double take. My head going back and forth between Kallen and Roman, like I'm fucking seeing double... because I am.

"What the fuck is going on here?" I ask, my throat dry, my heart racing.

"I see you've met my twin brother," Kallen winks, nodding towards the stranger I picked up on the side of the road—his twin fucking brother.

"Ahh, so that's why you grabbed my ass and asked if I wanted to fuck," Roman jokes, laughing as Kallen gives me a confused look.

"In my defense, I had no idea that there were two of you," I admit, taking a seat before I collapse from the shock still slapping me across the face.

"Skylar, you naughty little thing. If you wanna go out back and fuck, I'm down," Kallen coos, looking at me the way he did last night that caused us to end up in the same bed, fucking like goddamn bunnies.

"It's not funny. I feel played." I hang my head, feeling the embarrassment creeping to my cheeks.

"Im just fucking with you," he apologizes, putting his large, tattooed hand on the small of my back. "So how did you two meet?"

"My fucking bike broke down and she ended up stopping to give me a ride," Roman answers for me, for which I'm grateful.

"Oh, how cute. A fucking chick saved your day," Kallen laughs, trying to get a rise out of his brother. But it doesn't work.

"What's your poison?" I ask Kallen and Roman, ready to dive into the chaos of the night, needing a drink to ease the crippling anxiety.

"Surprise me," Roman replies nonchalantly, leaning over the counter, his confidence radiating.

"Same. I'll drink whatever you put in front of me," Kallen says, his confidence matching his brother's.

I order us shots of tequila—because why not go hard from the start? The bartender smirks knowingly, pouring the drinks with the swift precision of someone who's seen his fair share of wild nights. I place their shots in front of them and grab the other for myself, raising it in toast.

"To new friends and reckless nights," I declare, my gaze lingering a moment longer on both of them as we down the shots in unison.

"Damn, that burns," Roman coughs, wiping his mouth and laughing. "But I like it."

"Glad to hear that," I say, ordering us another round.

"Pussy," Kallen chimes in with playful banter.

A small part of me begins to buzz with excitement, not just from the alcohol but from the spontaneity of this unplanned adventure. Who would have thought my night would steer in a direction like this?

As laughter and banter flow between us, I begrudgingly push thoughts of everything else aside, at least for the moment. Roman is charming and engaging—everything I hadn't anticipated. Kallen is more blunt and opinionated, much different than his quieter brother.

In these haze-lit moments, I realize that maybe it's time to reconnect with whatever slivers of life and excitement I've tucked away since everything fell apart with Kaleb.

After a few more rounds and as the music shifts to something upbeat, I pull Roman onto the dance floor, wanting to feel the rush of the night surge through me. The crowd surrounds us, and I let loose, swaying my hips and allowing the rhythm to take over. And then Kallen joins us, both him and Roman matching my movements, their laughter blending with the beat, and amid the vibrant chaos, I finally feel free—more alive than ever.

The night unfolds in a whirlwind of music, movement, and unexpected connections. The tequila loosens my tongue, and my inhibitions melt away with each shot. Roman's touch on my waist as we dance is surprisingly gentle, a stark contrast to Kallen's more possessive grip. They're different, yet both undeniably captivating in their own ways. The initial shock of discovering Kallen's twin has faded, replaced by a thrilling sense of the absurd. This Valentine's Day, the one I swore I'd hate, is turning out to be anything but predictable.

Hours blur into a kaleidoscope of laughter, shared secrets whispered in crowded corners, and stolen glances across the dance floor. Kallen's playful competitiveness with his brother adds a layer of unexpected fun to the evening. They tease each other relentlessly, their banter a constant source of amusement. I find myself caught in the middle, enjoying the attention and the unexpected company. The initial awkwardness of the situation has completely vanished, replaced by a comfortable familiarity that surprises even me.

As the night deepens, the bar empties, leaving only a handful of die-hard revelers. The music softens, the atmosphere shifting from boisterous energy to a more intimate vibe. Roman pulls me aside, his eyes sparkling with a newfound intensity. He leans in, his breath warm against my ear.

"So," he whispers, his voice husky, "about that quickie you mentioned earlier."

A laugh escapes my lips, a mixture of surprise and exhilaration. I glance at Kallen, who's watching us with a smirk playing on his lips. He raises his glass in a silent toast, a silent acknowledgment of the unfolding chaos, then walks over to join us, yanking me out of his brother's embrace and into his.

The look the two of them share makes my palms sweaty and unwelcome butterflies swarm in my stomach. They're up to something, and fuck, I'm more than willing to find out what it is.

The initial anger and frustration I felt towards Kaleb have completely dissipated, replaced by a sense of liberation. I'm not dwelling on the past, not clinging to old resentments. Instead, I'm embracing the present, the intoxicating thrill of the unknown. The unexpected encounter with Roman, the revelation of Kallen's twin, the sheer absurdity of it all—it's a perfect storm.

The three of us end up leaving the bar together, the night air cool against my skin. The walk back to my apartment is filled with easy conversation, laughter, and a shared sense of adventure. The initial tension between Kallen and Roman has dissolved, replaced by a strange, unspoken understanding.

As we reach my apartment building, a strange sense of contentment washes over me. This Valentine's Day, the one I had vowed to despise, has become a night of unexpected twists, turns, and thrilling encounters. It's a night I won't soon forget, a night that has reminded me of the beauty of spontaneity, the thrill of the unexpected, and the intoxicating power of letting go.

"So," I whisper, my words slurring heavily as I look at both of them, holding onto the doorknob. "You two want to come up?" I wink, licking my lips, completely fucking obliterated.

They share a quick look, Kallen flashing me a wink as they take a step closer to me, the heat from their bodies engulfing me and stirring something deep inside my core. Roman cups one of my cheeks while Kallen grabs my throat like he did last night, both leaning in to whisper in my ears.

"What the fuck are we still doing down here, pretty girl?" Kallen growls in a sesuctive whisper, his breath kissing my skin like embers from a scorching fire.

Roman whispers next, making me tremble from the filth flowing from his mouth. "Yeah, little night rider, take us upstairs and show us if you can ride a cock as well as you can ride a bike."

Chapter Five
Night Rider

Skylar

The stairs seem to stretch endlessly—we can't get up them fast enough. We're already shedding clothes as the apartment door slams shut behind us. In the dim hallway, discarded garments mark our hurried path, like a trail of breadcrumbs. The alcohol surges through me, washing away everything but the present moment.

The aching in my body is momentarily forgotten, numbed by the liquor, though I know the reckoning will come tenfold tomorrow—especially with two of them.

What the fuck am I doing?

Inside my room, I close the door and turn to find the twins sprawled on my bed, naked and bathed in the moon's silvery light streaming in from the window behind them. Their muscular forms glow, and their intricate tattoos captivate my gaze. I stand mesmerized, mouth open, heart racing, and pussy, fucking dripping.

They're both covered in them. They both have their nipples pierced. I know for a fact Kallen has his dick pierced, and from the looks of it, Roman does too, and it makes me lick my lips as my eyes dart between both of them, trying to compare sizes like a fucking pervert.

"Come on, Night Rider," Roman urges, wrapping his large hand around his cock, stroking slowly with his hungry eyes on me. "Take it all off and don't be shy."

"You shouldn't be shy anyway," Kallen interjects, grinning as he too begins to stroke his own cock. "Not after the way I fucked you last night."

Roman glares at him, a spark of jealousy gleaming in his drunken green eyes. A quick smile flashes across his glistening lips after he licks them, recovering the look of jealousy quickly like a pro.

They say twins do everything alike, so I stand here wondering if they fuck alike too.

Still in a heavy daze, mesmerized by their beautiful naked bodies and rather large cocks, I lick my dry lips and slowly step closer, feeling like I'm being pushed rather than walking on my own. I reach behind my body and slide my fingers underneath my bra strap, undoing the clasp my first try, which never happens. Truth be told, I usually turn my bra around to the front to clasp and unclasp it because it's fucking impossible to do behind my back.

Not tonight, it isn't.

Trying to be sexy, I slowly pull off my bra, letting it dangle from my fingers in front of me, my tits on full display for the fucking gods in front of me. My nipples are so hard my piercings hurt, which is strange, but it gives a tingling sensation that literally makes them throb with anticipation. I drop my bra and take another step, grinning at the twins.

"Fuck, you've got some nice tits, Night Rider," Roman growls, hunger etched on his face, his hand moving faster now.

"Now your thong," Kallen urges, leaning back a bit as he continues to stroke himself. "Take it the fuck off."

"Please?" I huff, putting my hands on my hips and pushing my tits out, teasing them as much as I can.

He smirks, flashing a seductive wink. "Please," he coos, drawing out the word. "Take your fucking thong off."

I smirk back, hooking my thumbs under the thin black band of my thong on each hip, slowly pushing it down, and watching their eyes widen. Stepping out of it, I kick it toward them and take one more step closer, now standing directly in front of them, mere inches away.

The sound of skin on skin echoes, their hands pumping rapidly as they grow impatient by the second. I lean down in front of Roman, wrapping my hand around his, helping him jerk himself off. My lips collide with his, and it feels like the world stops, our tongues eagerly thrusting in and out of each other's mouths while Kallen watches.

Roman's kiss is more soft, more delicate than Kallen's, but still just as hot and delicious. He manages to clasp his hand around my hip and tug me onto his lap, his thick cock slapping my pussy as I fall right onto it. Still lost in the kiss, I feel the bed rise beside us as Kallen gets up and stands behind me, his lips trailing scorching kisses along my spine and setting all my nerve endings on fucking fire.

I shiver as he brushes the hair away from the back of my neck, putting it all to one side. He glides his tongue along my nape, stepping closer so his cock pokes against my ass, making me jump. Breaking the kiss with Roman, I turn my head to the side to meet Kallen's gaze, and he crashes his mouth onto mine before I can catch my breath.

While I'm occupied, Roman takes advantage and begins rubbing rough circles over my clit as my pussy drips all over him. His other hand reaches up and cups my breast, greedily kneading it, and his mouth locks around my other one, his tongue flicking my nipple and making it even harder.

"Oh, fuck," I whimper against Kallen's mouth, slowly breaking the kiss.

He grins, his body flush against mine, and rubs his dick up and down my ass, the tip prodding at my hole and making me tense.

"Uh uh, don't do that," he tells me, pushing on my lower back so I'm leaning on his brother, our chests colliding. "It'll hurt more."

I roll my eyes, grinding on Roman, growing needier by the second. "I've been fucked in the ass before…it's just been a while," I admit, grinning until I feel my dimples popping.

"Well damn, say no more," he growls, winking again as he—without warning—thrusts his dick into my ass with only the wetness from my pussy for lube.

"Shit!" I shriek, feeling the burn for the first few strokes, my nails digging into Roman's chest.

They both laugh, giving me that look that sucked me in from the beginning. Roman grabs my jaw and forcefully jerks my head in his direction, pushing the tip of his cock between my pussy lips until he finds my entrance, then thrusts his hips upward and slides inside of me the rest of the way. I gasp, throw my head back, and squeeze my eyes shut, never in my life feeling this full. I freeze, two cocks inside of me, not sure how to move… and they can tell too.

"Come on, Night Rider, bounce on my cock while my brother fucks your ass. Make a game of it," Roman demands, a playful grin dancing on his full lips. "Bounce as hard as you can without letting his cock slip out of your ass."

"Think you can do it?" Kallen asks, holding my hips firmly as he pulls me back onto his cock.

"Only one way to find out," I tease, sitting up carefully, feeling both of them stretch me out in ways that I've only dreamed of.

Looking into Roman's eyes, I rake my nails down his sculpted chest, tracing over his muscles as I use my knees to bounce, sliding up and down on his thick cock. I push my ass back and my chest forward, putting an arch in my back that allows the twins' cocks to slide deeper inside me. They both growl, hissing through clenched teeth as I ride, trying to live up to the nickname Roman gave me.

Kallen yanks on my hair as he pounds into my ass, jerking my head backward, exposing my neck to his brother. Taking advantage, Roman unexpectedly snatches my throat, squeezing hard and cutting off my airflow, only leaving me the smallest amount of room to breathe.

"Fuck, you're so good at this," Kallen praises me, licking the shell of my ear, his hot breath making me tremble.

"Have you taken two cocks like this before?" Roman asks, choking me, his other hand pinching my clit to get a rise out of me.

I whimper, trying to keep up with their rapid movements and deep thrusts, feeling like I'm about to fucking explode. He twists my clit, making me yelp, and then slaps my pussy like it's a disobedient child.

"Fucking answer me," he commands in a deep, dominating voice that shocks me.

"No," I pant, swallowing against the palm of his hand. "I haven't."

"Could've fooled me, pretty girl," Kallen says, fucking my ass with sharp, deep strokes, his cock stretching out my muscles and making them clench at the same time.

Roman pulls me down by my throat, putting his mouth on mine and kissing me again. My pussy tightens around his cock as I grind, rolling my hips feverishly, feeling my climax approaching. I moan into his mouth, his hand tangling in my hair, and ride even faster.

"Are you about to come, pretty girl?" Kallen asks, sliding out of my ass and brutally slamming back in, a hot gush of fluid spilling inside of me.

"Yes," I moan, biting Roman's lip as his brother empties himself into my ass, holding my hips in place until he shudders as the last drop finds its way with the rest.

"Come for us, Night Rider," Roman urges, thrusting his hips to meet my pelvis as I slam down on his cock.

Kallen stays buried in my ass, not letting my hips go, kissing the side of my neck and grazing his teeth across my skin. I cry out, throwing my head back once more as my pussy squeezes Roman's cock in a heartbeat rhythm, soaking it with my release. And all of a sudden Kallen pulls out of my ass, giving it a sharp slap that instantly burns my cheek.

"Push it out, pretty girl," he instructs, still behind me watching his brother's cock slide in and out of my pussy. "I want to watch my cum drip out of your ass while you come."

I scrunch my nose as I watch Roman grin, feeling his dick pulsing inside me. I do as I'm told and push, feeling the hot fluid drip out of me and slide down my pussy, mixing with my cum as it coats his brother's cock.

"Now that's a pretty creampie," he chuckles, giving my ass another hard slap in the same spot, ripping a yelp from my dry throat.

"Ever had cum from two dicks inside you before?" Roman asks with his brow arched, his hands holding my hips as he begins to slam me down as hard as he can. "At the same time..."

"No," I answer right away, remembering what he did when I didn't answer before.

"Well now you have." He smirks, sending me over the edge along with him.

I come, and I come hard, soaking him as he fills me up, his and his brother's cum being pushed back inside me each time I sink on his cock. But I don't even care right now; it feels so good. My body aches with need, pleasure coursing through my veins like a drug. My pussy throbs as Roman slams me down over and over on his dick until he's empty, sticky cum from all three of us coating my pussy lips and mixing inside of me. I collapse on the bed on my back, my chest rising and falling frantically as I try to catch my breath.

The twins fall beside me, the three of us staring at the glow and the dark stars on my ceiling as the noise from outside returns and our little bubble of pleasure bursts, snapping me back to reality.

Fuck. What the fuck did I just do?

My cheeks heat, a blush evident across them. I close my eyes as the twins turn to look at me, their warm, strong hands caressing my naked body, almost putting me to sleep. But I fight it. They can't sleep here. I don't do that shit. If we fuck, you leave when we're done because I'm not trying to catch feelings.

Feelings lead to heartbreak, and I can't go through another.

I sit up so fast I get dizzy, the room spinning before my eyes as a slight ringing pierces my ears. I hang my head and close my eyes, waiting for the discomfort to subside.

"You alright, Skylar?" Kallen asks, his voice soothing, much different from the dominant tone he had with me moments earlier.

Roman rubs my back, gently showering my shoulder with wet kisses, trying to comfort me from the unknown.

"I'm fine," I whisper, trying hard to be convincing. "Tired though."

"Then lay down. We'll be right here if you need anything," Roman tells me, and my heart sinks.

How the fuck am I supposed to tell them to leave? Especially after the fucking night we just had.

I stay quiet, hoping they'll get the hint and get their asses dressed. But they don't.

"Listen," I begin, speaking softly. "I have a lot to do tomorrow, so I need to get some sleep tonight. If ya'll stay, we all know that isn't going to happen," I chuckle, giving both of them a smile.

"Alright, we'll go, but can we see you tomorrow?" Kallen gives me a sweet look that tugs at my heartstrings, his green eyes piercing right into my soul.

"Yeah, it won't be until tomorrow night because I have plans with my mother, but I'll text you when I'm done."

Satisfied with my answer, the twins finally get off my bed and kiss me goodbye, gathering their discarded clothes in the hallway and getting dressed in the living room before leaving my apartment, locking the door behind them.

I lay back down, not bothering to get dressed. I stare out my window and light a cigarette, trying to process what just fucking happened. But only one thing keeps coming to me, and that's the fact that I'm now a fucking whore for fucking twins at the same time.

At least I checked something off my bucket list, and to be honest, I don't ever have to see them again if I don't want to.

Chapter Six
The Shocker

Skylar

After attempting to sleep as long as I could, the relentless dinging of my phone finally drives me to frustration, compelling me to awaken before I was ready. Notifications inundate my phone, each ping pricking my curiosity—I can't help but wonder what's fucking happening.

As I sit up, I feel utterly shattered; my body cracks and pops like a creaky old house, making me feel like I've aged decades overnight. I knew I would be sore, but this shit is a whole new fucking level of discomfort.

The sun blazes through the window, blinding me—how did I forget to close the blinds? My eyes burn like I've been caught in the light of day, as a vampire might. A chilling breeze drifts through the open window, harshly reminding me of still being naked. I wrap a blanket around myself, light a cigarette, and reach for my phone to check the time.

2:34 PM.

Great, I've managed to sleep away half the day.

I shrug it off and swipe my phone to life. Tapping on Instagram, my jaw drops at the first image that appears on my feed: over a hundred notifications awaiting me. My stomach knots and a lump forms in my throat as I read the caption on my mother's post, anger boiling within me.

The picture features her hand, showcasing an enormous engagement ring that steals the spotlight, with the caption that reads, "I said yes!" As I digest the information, shock washes over me, hitting like a fucking brick wall.

He fucking proposed to her? On Valentine's Day? How incredibly cliché. But what utterly baffles me is their fucking audacity—posting this on social media without telling me first.

Fuming, I immediately navigate to my mother's profile and hit the block button, then throw my phone across the room in a fit of rage, hoping it shatters upon impact.

It doesn't. Just my fucking luck.

Knowing I'll have to face both of them at dinner in a few hours only fuels my anger with every passing second. My mother is fully aware of my temperament; she knows I won't hold my tongue. She understands that I'm about to unleash a storm of anger on her and Kent, and I'll rip them both a new asshole.

I throw off the blanket and storm out of my room, naked and determined to shower—I need to wash away the remnants of last night's indiscretions. Ironically, all I can think about are the twins, and now I'm itching to call them more than ever. I need an escape, a release, before dinner so that I can at least partially temper my rage.

Stepping into the shower, I stand beneath the scalding water, allowing it to wash over me while the heat turns my skin red and raw. The water does little to soothe the burning rage simmering beneath my skin. The twins are still on my mind, their faces a hazy memory of last night's tangled limbs and breathless whispers. I scrub harder, the rough washcloth a poor substitute for the raw, visceral anger I feel. Kent. The audacity. My mother, so fucking self-absorbed, so utterly oblivious to the hurt she inflicts. Fucking Valentine's Day. Of all the goddamn days. The cliché is almost more infuriating than the betrayal. *Almost.*

The hot water finally begins to lose its sting, replaced by a dull ache in my muscles. I turn the tap to cold, the shock jolting me back to the present. I need a plan. A strategy. I can't just unleash a torrent of fury; I need to be calculated, precise. I need to hurt them as much as they've hurt me. The thought is both exhilarating and terrifying.

Toweling off, I dress quickly, choosing something sharp and unforgiving—tight black jeans, a tight black crop shirt, and boots that make a satisfying thud on the wooden floor. I need to look the part—the part of the furious daughter—the one who won't be silenced. I glance at my reflection—pale, eyes bloodshot, but there's a glint of something else there, something cold and hard. This isn't just anger anymore; it's something colder, something sharper. Revenge.

I grab my phone; the cracked screen is a testament to my earlier outburst. I don't bother to repair it. Instead, I open my contacts and scroll to the twins' number. This isn't an escape; it's a weapon. A carefully chosen weapon to be wielded with precision. I press call, the ringing a counterpoint to the steady beat of my own heart. This is going to be a long, brutal evening… after I hopefully get my brains fucked out of me first.

Roman answers on the third ring, putting his phone on speaker, his and Kallen's voices a welcome balm to my simmering rage. We exchange breathless greetings, the usual playful banter a thin veil over the underlying tension. I don't mention my mother's engagement, not yet. Instead, I focus on arranging a rendezvous—a pre-dinner meeting that will serve as both distraction and preparation. Their apartment is close, a quick bike ride away. We agree to meet in an hour.

The ride is a blur of angry thoughts and frantic planning. The image of my mother's ring flashes in my mind, a constant reminder of the betrayal. I clench my fists, knuckles turning white. Parking my bike, I climb off, strutting my way up the path to the door of the complex. Of course, the twins are waiting for me at the door.

"Look who couldn't stay away," Roman jokes, flashing me the same wink he kept giving me last night.

"Fuck off, I'm just here for one thing," I snap, giving both of them a sultry look that needs no other explanation.

"Fuck, Skylar, you're looking fine, pretty girl," Kallen says, taking in my tight, black outfit, completely inappropriate for a dinner with my mother, her boyfriend, and his kids, but that was the whole point.

"Oh, this old thing," I tease, finishing my cigarette before following them inside.

The twins' apartment is a haven of controlled chaos, a familiar comfort in the midst of my turmoil. We drink, we smoke, we talk—mostly them about how they're liking it here since they moved. When my turn comes around, they listen intently as I pour out my fury without telling them the full nature of my anger, my voice rising and falling with the tide of my emotions. They offer words of comfort, but mostly they just listen, their presence a silent affirmation of my pain. Their understanding is a lifeline, a temporary reprieve from the storm raging inside me.

"What can we do?" Roman asks, handing me a beer that I accept gratefully.

"Fuck me like you did last night," I admit, hoping they're wanting it as much as I am.

"Say no more," Kallen says, standing up and facing me as I lean my back against the balcony.

He tugs my waistband, jerking me toward him as we back up to the glass door. He pushes my pants down and takes them all the way off, lifting me into his arms as he places his back against the door, my legs wrapping around his waist.

Roman gets behind me, unlike last night when his brother was. Their zippers lower in unison, and their pants come down to their knees. Roman holds me, my back resting against his chest while my legs still lock around Kallen's waist. Each of them takes turns kissing me, my head being jerked from all sides to accommodate their kisses.

Kallen enters me first, using his knees to thrust up into my pussy, fucking me gently while I lean against Roman for leverage. He kisses my neck, not shy about leaving dark bite marks behind, looking like hickey central—even fucking better for tonight.

After Kallen fucks me with a few deep, dominating thrusts, he pulls out of me, and Roman slips in from behind, slightly pushing me forward against his brother to get a better angle. They leave my ass alone and take turns fucking my pussy, leaving me whimpering each time one of them pulls out and then moaning every time one of them thrusts back in.

My pussy is on fire, soaked and needy like its never been before. I cling to Kallen's shoulder with one hand while I grip the back of Roman's neck, refusing to let either of them go. I bounce on their cocks while in their arms, the fear of being dropped not a worry in my mind.

My skin is covered in wetness from their incessant kisses, bite marks, and bruises decorating my neck and chest, a testament to their insatiable hunger.

"Yes, fuck, yes," I moan loudly, coming on Kallen's cock as he fills me with his.

Before I can finish, he slides out of me and Roman slides in, letting me finish showering his cock with my cum as he takes his turn and empties himself inside of me too. Much like last night, I have both of their seeds inside of me, and they both have mine coating their dicks. It's become normal now, in just two encounters, but it's something that I can't seem to walk away from.

If fucking twin brothers categorize me as a slut, then I'm the biggest slut there is, and I could give two flying fucks about it.

By the time we're done, spent, satisfied, and completely empty, the sun has fully set and the night chill sweeps across our half-naked bodies, urging us to get dressed quicker. We sit on the balcony, smoking a blunt that we pass back and forth, nothing but the bustling city floating between us. I'm all talked out, all fucked out, fully satiated.

A quick glance at the time and my stomach sinks, knowing I have to head out to make it to dinner on time.

"Fuck, I gotta get going," I mumble, sighing heavily.

"Yeah, we're gonna head out too. But hey, I was serious; if you need us to come get you out of there, all you have to do is call, Night Rider," Roman says, winking, giving me another kiss that almost makes me change my mind about going.

A chilling calm descends. The initial fire of rage has been tempered, replaced by a cold, calculating determination. The twins, sensing the shift, exchange a knowing glance.

"Call or text us if you need anything, especially if you can't take it and need one of us to pick you up," Kallen says, kissing me on the cheek while his brother kisses my other one.

"I will. If you don't hear from me, I'm probably in jail for beating the shit out of my mother." I wink, smirking deadly as they walk me to my bike.

I swing my leg over the seat, put my helmet on, and start my bike, giving them one last look before speeding away, the familiar hum and vibrations putting my anxiety at ease.

But it isn't going to last for long.

I opted for the longest route to the restaurant, relishing the thought of annoying my mother by being late. I also needed to calm my fucking nerves, and riding my bike is the only remedy for that—well, aside from the extra Xanax I've already taken today.

When I finally arrive—thirty minutes late—I feel a surprising sense of relief from the ride. Reluctantly, I dismount, adjusting my outfit to expose as much skin as possible without appearing completely nude.

Strutting into the restaurant, I can't help but beam with a freshly fucked glow on my face, a wide grin giving away my stoned state. It's the only fucking way I can endure this dinner without losing complete control—and even then, I can't make any fucking promises.

As I make my way through the bustling crowd, I hear my mother's laughter ring out from across the room, a sound that grates on my nerves like nails on a chalkboard. The closer I get, the more anxious I become, eventually glancing up to spot her enormous ring before anything else.

I shake my head as I approach the table, where she and Kent are seated, his sons with their backs to me. For a moment, I forget they'd be joining us tonight, too wrapped up in the surprise engagement and the fact that no one had thought to inform me.

"Skylar, you're nearly forty-five minutes late," my mother says, shooting me a look that used to make me shit my pants when I was younger.

But it doesn't have the same impact anymore.

"Sweetheart, just be glad she made it at all," Kent chimes in, flashing me a smile reminiscent of the one my mother fell for—a familiar grin that eludes my memory.

"Lucky for you, I even fucking showed up," I retort, snapping at her, accidentally grabbing the attention of the two quiet guys across from them.

As they turn to face me, my heart sinks and my jaw drops; I'm frozen in place, struggling to find my voice, utterly fucking bewildered.

"Ah, Skylar, I'd like you to meet my sons," Kent cheerfully announces, and my gaze locks onto those two sets of striking green eyes that seem to cut right through me. "They're twins—Kallen and Roman."

Of course, Kallen winks at me, a playful, mischievous glint in his eyes that leaves me speechless. Roman appears shy but happy, a contrast to Kallen's boldness.

Kallen rises and sits in the seat next to him, encouraging me to sit between him and Roman.

"Come on, Skylar, get to know your new stepbrothers." My mother smirks, sipping her wine slowly as she observes my reaction.

My new stepbrothers... my twin stepbrothers. The same fucking twins I spent the last two nights tangled up with in ways that send a flush to my cheeks just thinking about it. What on earth did I do to fucking deserve this? It feels as if Cupid has a personal fucking vendetta against me—or perhaps someone up there enjoys this chaotic twist of fate. Why else would this shit be happening?

I sit down, holding my breath for what's to come. I have no idea how things are going to go from here, but knowing that I've been fucking my stepbrothers, I can only assume shit is going to be awkward. Right?

Acknowledgements

Thank you all for reading my little Valentine's Day Novella. Check out the other 6 books in the
Wicked Meet Cute Series; you won't be disappointed!
I want to thank all the authors and wonderful ladies who brought this little project together. I had
so much fun working with you all.
Thank you to my Smutty Fucker teams for promoting and hyping the shit out of it, and of course
for reading.
I hope it gave you at least a little smile, especially to those who aren't huge fans of the holiday.

Also By K.M. Rogness

Other books by KM ROGNESS:
Trick or Treat
Trick or Treat: the alternate ending
Breaking Boston
Drowning
Little Psycho: Book 1 in the Killer Kids thrillogy
Psycho Boys: Book 2 in the Killer Kids thrillogy
Psycho Killers: Book 3 in the Killer kids thrillogy (coming March 31st)
Touchdowns and Tinsel
Unwrapping Ember

Give me a follow on Amazon to stay up to date with all new releases: KM ROGNESS
IG: @darksmutauthor_kaseyr
Website: https://kmrogness.com
Scan the QR code below to find my work, order signed copies, and more!

Stay dark, stay twisted, stay smutty —Kasey

www.ingramcontent.com/pod-product-compliance
Lightning Source LLC
LaVergne TN
LVHW061048070526
838201LV00074B/5222